DRACULA

by Ian Thorne

Macmillan Publishing Company
866 Third Avenue
New York, NY 10022
Collier Macmillan Canada, Inc.
Printed in the United States of America
First Edition
20 19 18 17 16 15 14 13 12 11 10 9
Reprinted 1982
Library of Congress Catalog Card Number: 76-051145.
ISBN 0-913-94067-4
Design—Doris Woods and Randal M. Heise.

PHOTOGRAPHIC CREDITS

Forrest J. Ackerman: Cover, 21, 22; American-International Pictures — 41, 42; ABC-TV: 44, 45; CBS-TV: 46, 47; Hammer Films: 2; Prana-Film: 29; Universal Pictures: 6, 9, 14, 17, 20; Warner Bros.: 43.
Metro-Goldwyn-Mayer: 10
Vincent Miranda, Jr.: Hammer Films: 34, 36, 37; MGM: 30, 31; Prana-Film: 28; Universal Pictures: 13, 32, 33, 38, 39
Publication Associates: 25
Romanian Ministry of Tourism: 24
UPI: 26

Published by
CRESTWOOD HOUSE, INC.
Macmillan Publishing Company
866 Third Avenue
New York, N.Y. 10022
Printed in the United States of America

DRACULA

Bela Lugosi, as Count Dracula, welcomes Renfield, played by Dwight Frye.

People went to the movie expecting to be scared. And Dracula didn't disappoint them!

The story began in mist and darkness.

An Englishman named Renfield came to the wild mountain country of Transylvania. He was to meet a nobleman, Count Dracula, who wished to buy a place in England.

Renfield stayed at an inn in the mountains. The people at the inn were horrified when Renfield told them he was on the way to Castle Dracula. They warned him not to go there, but they would not say why.

"I have important business with Count Dracula," Renfield insisted.

The innkeeper's wife took a cross from around her neck and gave it to Renfield. "Then wear this," she insisted. "For your mother's sake!"

The coach came to the inn. Renfield began the last part of his journey. Faster and faster the horses galloped, dragging the coach deep into the eerie mountains.

Renfield leaned out the window to ask the driver to slow down. But he saw no driver — only a small creature flying above the frightened horses, urging them on.

It was a bat.

Finally, the coach arrived at Castle Dracula. But the place was in ruins! "Surely," Renfield thought, "no one could live in such a place." The walls were crumbling. Huge spider webs hung from the arches.

A figure appeared at the top of a worn stone staircase. It was a man in clean, crisp evening dress, wearing a satin lined cloak.

"I am . . . Dracula!" he said, smiling. "I bid you welcome. Enter freely and of your own will!"

Amazed, Renfield followed the Count into the castle. Dracula walked through a great spider web but the web was not torn by his passing.

The count offered Renfield a drink but he would not take a glass with his guest. "I never drink . . . wine," Dracula explained.

Later, Renfield happened to cut his finger. The sight of blood worked a strange change in Count Dracula. He came at Renfield, eyes shining. The Englishman fell back and the cross he wore came into view.

Dracula shrank back. He left Renfield alone. While the puzzled and frightened Englishman tried to rest, three weird women came into the room. Closer and closer they came. What did they want? They wanted him . . .

A great bat came flapping into the room. It drove the weird women away. Poor Renfield fell down, fainting from fright. In an instant, the bat disappeared. In its place was the smiling figure of Count Dracula. He was ready to claim his victim!

Once bitten by the vampire, Renfield became Dracula's slave. The evil Count wanted to go to England. Coffins, filled with Transylvanian earth, were taken to a ship and loaded on board. One of the coffins contained something else as well as dirt. Renfield guarded it well.

When the ship landed in England, the horrified people at the dock found that the entire crew was dead. Only Renfield, now a raving madman, was left alive. Of course, there also were the boxes of earth neatly addressed to Count Dracula at his new home of Carfax Abbey.

The abbey was in ruins. It looked a lot like Castle Dracula! For that reason, the evil Count felt right at home when he came out of one of the earth-filled coffins. Dracula had worn out his welcome in Transylvania, but England was a fresh new place for him to work. He got down to business at once.

Nearby was the private mental hospital of Dr. Seward. Mad Renfield had been taken there. Dracula went to call on his new neighbor.

He brought a present. "I have found a farmhand lying in the road," Dracula explained. "He needs your care."

Dr. Seward and his lovely daughter, Mina, looked at the man. His body was drained of blood! And there were fang marks on his throat.

Mina gave a cry of fear. "I saw a great bat outside the window," she told her father. "And the bat's eyes — they were the same as those of Dracula!"

Dr. Seward tried to calm his daughter. "I will send for Professor Van Helsing," he said. "He will know what to do about this."

Professor Van Helsing promised to come to England from Holland. Meanwhile, Dracula kept busy and took as his next victim a friend of Mina's named Lucy. Lucy, bitten again and again by the vampire, was turned into a vampire herself.

Dracula shows his mastery over the luckless Renfield. Lucy (Frances Dade) had become a vampire.

Jonathan Harker (David Manners) recoils from a bat while Mina (Helen Chandler) begins to fall under Dracula's spell.

Then Dracula began to follow Mina. The young woman told her fears to her fiance, Jonathan Harker. She felt terror and a strange sleepiness. She was losing control of her will. Dracula was calling her and she wanted to go to him.

By this time, Professor Van Helsing had come to stay with the Sewards. He was an expert on supernatural matters. He explained to Dr. Seward and Harker that Count Dracula was a vampire — an "undead" monster that fed on human blood. Persons who died from the vampire's bite became vampires themselves. Dracula would have to be destroyed.

Van Helsing knew that Dracula was after Mina. He tried to protect her by hanging garlic flowers around her room. He did that because garlic is said to be a vampire repellent.

When Mina went to bed, she seemed to have a strange dream. "Open the window!" urged a voice. In a trance, she rose and took away the garlic. Next, she opened the window.

A huge bat flew into the room. And then Count Dracula stood before the bewitched girl. She felt blackness swell up around her.

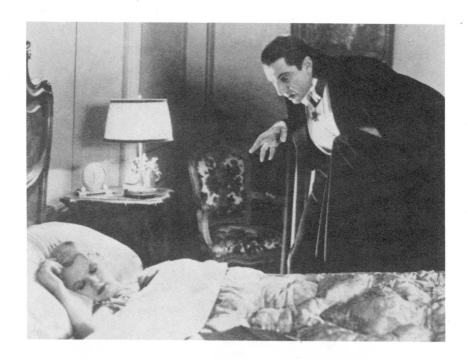

Professor Van Helsing (Edward van Sloan) drives off Dracula with a cross.

Mina had suffered the bite of the vampire. However, she was saved from Lucy's fate because Dracula did not take all of her blood. Not that time!

Mina's fiance, Harker, was powerless to protect her from the menace. Her father could not break the Count's spell either. Each night, Mina seemed to hear Dracula calling . . . calling. She had to go to him.

Only Professor Van Helsing had the knowledge that could destroy the vampire. He made his plans to trap Count Dracula.

Van Helsing and Dracula met. The clever professor offered Dracula a cigarette from a case with a mirror in the lid. Dracula did not cast any reflection in the mirror! It was proof the Count was one of the undead.

Furious, Dracula tried to attack Professor Van Helsing, but the scientist pulled out a cross and held it up. The emblem of goodness drove Dracula back and he fled.

The vampire returned to Carfax Abbey, to the coffin full of earth where he rested during daylight.

Dracula's power over Mina was now very great. He called out to her and she had to leave her home and go off through the misty night toward the abbey.

When Van Helsing, Harker and Dr. Seward discovered that Mina had gone, they hurried after her. But what if they were too late? What if Dracula had already turned the girl into a vampire as he had done with poor Lucy?

Van Helsing knew there was only one way to destroy Dracula or any other vampire. The vampire had to be discovered in his coffin, during daylight, while he was sleeping and helpless. A wooden stake would have to be driven through his heart.

The men searched the abbey for Dracula's coffin. Just as the sun began to come up, they found two coffins.

One contained the body of Dracula, but Dr. Seward and Harker could not bear to open the other. What if Mina lay inside?

Van Helsing said to Harker, "Go and find a stone. We will use it to drive home the stake."

Harker stumbled out of the abbey to look for a stone.

Harker wandered, sick with fear for Mina. But suddenly he saw a white figure. It was his bride-to-be! She was walking in the sunlight — alive. She had not been turned into a vampire. She was safe.

Professor Van Helsing did not wait for Harker to return. He found a stone himself. He did what had to be done.

As the stake pierced the vampire's heart, Mina winced, and then she was free. Dracula's spell over her was broken.

Professor Van Helsing came into the sunlight to meet them. "Dracula is dead forever," he said.

Almost in the drawing of a breath, Dracula's whole body crumbled to dust . . .

Bram Stoker, author of Dracula, from a photo taken in 1906.

BRINGING VAMPIRES TO LIFE

The story of Dracula was first told by Bram Stoker, an Irish-born writer. He was a newspaper editor who wrote thrillers for the popular papers during the late 1800's. One of his close friends was a professor from the University of Budapest in Hungary. This man told Stoker about the vampire legends of Transylvania.

Stoker went to the best libraries in London and studied all about vampires and about the history of Transylvania. Many European countries had vampire legends. The vampires of Transylvania were undead monsters that rose from the grave and tried to steal your beauty or your strength. Or they might try to kill you, unless you chased them away with garlic.

The vampire legends of Greece featured blood-sucking monsters. Stoker put together both of these legends in his story.

The writer also studied vampire bats. These are small flying mammals with bodies about the size of mice. They live only in Central and South America. A bat will come up to a sleeping animal and make a cut with its sharp teeth. Then it laps up the blood. The little bat does not take much blood; but it can spread rabies, so it is dangerous.

Stoker used the vampire bat as part of his story, too.

This portrait of Vlad Tepes hangs in a museum in Romania.

The idea for the vampire hero, Dracula, came from a real person. Prince Vlad Dracula was born in the Transylvania town of Sighisoara about 1430. His second name was a kind of family title, meaning "dragon's son." The prince's father was Vlad Dracula, a member of the Order of the Dragon of the Holy Roman Empire. Members of the Dragon Society fought the Turks, who had attacked Europe. Both Dracula and his father took part in the fight. In fact, Dracula is considered a national hero in Romania today because he helped save his country from Turkish victory.

Prince Dracula was very brave, but he had a darker side to his nature as well. He was a mass murderer who liked to torture his victims to death by driving wooden stakes through them. The impaled bodies were then set up like a ghastly fence in order to frighten Turkish invaders.

Dracula tortured and killed his own people as well as Turks. If anyone made him unhappy in any way, he would have the person impaled. On one day in 1459, he murdered 10,000 citizens of the town of Sibiu. At Brasov, thousands of people were impaled and set up around a place where Dracula and his men held a merry outdoor feast.

Transylvania means "beyond the mountains." Dracula was born in Sighisoara, north of the Transylvanian Alps. He had palaces in both Sibiu and Tirgoviste, as well as his castle, which is in ruins. Dracula died in an ambush just outside Bucharest. He is believed buried in a monastery at Snagov. Romania offers tours of "Dracula Country."

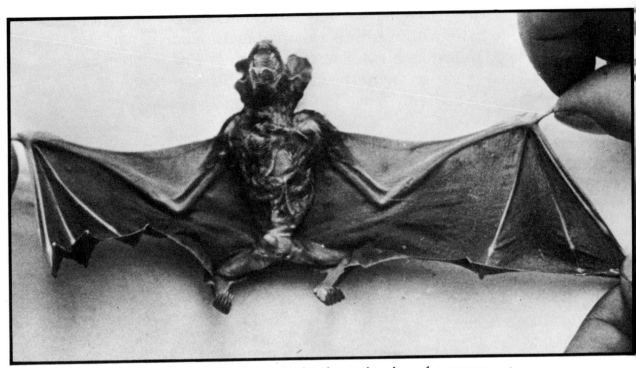

The real vampire bat has a body about the size of a mouse.

Dracula's cruel acts made him famous. Mothers throughout Europe and in the Turkish Empire used the name of the dreadful prince to frighten their naughty children.

Dracula built a castle at the headwaters of the Argas River. It was partly destroyed by the Turks in 1462 and the Prince had to flee for his life. He went northward and was taken prisoner by Hungarians. For the next 12 years, he was a prisoner.

Dracula was released in 1474 as the Turks mounted a new offensive into Europe. He died during a battle against the invaders in 1476.

Prince Vlad is known to historians as Vlad Tepes (TSEP-esh) — meaning "Vlad the Impaler." No one ever accused the real prince of being a vampire. This is Bram Stoker's invention.

The author may have taken his "eternal youth" idea for vampires from another real person. Elizabeth Bathory was a Transylvanian countess famed for her beauty. When she began to grow old, she went insane. She believed the blood of girls would restore her youth. She murdered about 50 maidens and bathed in their blood before her deeds were discovered. She was walled up alive in her castle and died in 1614.

Elizabeth Bathory (1560-1614) was called the Blood Countess.

Bram Stoker's novel, Dracula, was published in 1897. It was a great success, and it still can be found on the shelves of libraries everywhere.

The first motion picture versions of Dracula were made in 1921. The only one of these films that can be seen today is Nosferatu, a classic of silent horror. The title means "vampire" in Romanian.

The movie was made by a German, F. W. Murnau. He changed the names of all the characters and changed the places from Transylvania to Germany. Dracula is called Count Orlock. He is shown as an evil inhuman with a bald head, pointed ears, and claw-tip-ped fingers. Even today, the sight of actor Max Schreck as Orlock is enough to freeze one's blood!

Nosferatu stalks his victim.

When sunlight strikes Nosferatu, he fades like mist.

Murnau's Nosferatu added two bits of vampire lore that Bram Stoker did not have in his original story. Count Orlock had pointed teeth. (And what modern vampire would be seen without fangs?) At the end of Nosferatu, the vampire is destroyed by rays of sunlight. He fades away into a mist at the end of the film.

In 1924, Hamilton Deane adapted Dracula into a stage play which became a hit, playing for years. The New York play starred a Hungarian actor named Bela Lugosi — who would become well known as the first Dracula of the American screen.

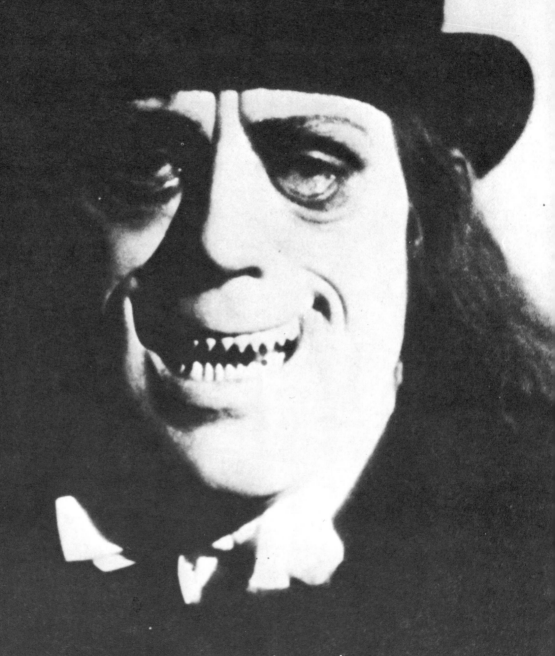

Lon Chany, Sr. starred in London After Midnight *(1927), later remade as* Mark *of the Vampire.*

The American film, Dracula, was first shown in 1931. It still can be seen today, and it is still frightening. Bela Lugosi, who played the Count in the stage play, repeated his role on the screen. He was the perfect Dracula — tall, sleek, with intent green eyes and a hypnotic smile.

Lugosi was born in the town of Lugoj in Transylvania! He said later, "I was born in almost the exact location of the Dracula story. I know that certain things which are looked upon as mere superstition are really based on facts!"

He may have believed what he was saying. At any rate, the Dracula character he created is unforgettable.

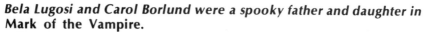

Bela Lugosi and Carol Borlund were a spooky father and daughter in Mark of the Vampire.

Many other vampire movies were made after the success of Dracula. Lugosi starred in several of them. Sadly enough, he was "typecast" as a vampire and rarely played any other role on the screen. When he died in 1956, he was buried, as he had asked, in his black Dracula cloak lined with red satin.

In 1935, Lugosi starred in Mark of the Vampire. He played Count Mora, a ghostly vampire who haunts a castle together with his daughter, Luna. This movie had a lot of scary scenes but it disappointed some people who saw it.

Lon Chaney, Jr. makes an entrance in Son of Dracula.

Dracula's daughter cremates the body of her father. She tried in vain to become human once more.

Among the more interesting vampire movies were Dracula's Daughter (1936), starring the icy Gloria Holden, and Son of Dracula (1943), starring Lon Chaney, Jr. Chaney's father had played a vampire character in the silent film, London After Midnite (1927).

Return of the Vampire (1944) starred Lugosi as a Dracula-like Count who stalks the English countryside. But this time, the vampire has a rival! A werewolf is also on the prowl. The two monsters quarrel over their victims until they destroy each other in a frightening finish to the film.

Christopher Lee in Hammer's
Horror of Dracula.

The vampire films of older days were scary because of the things they didn't show. You had to use your imagination to picture the vampire biting the victim. You might hear the blows as the vampire died with a stake through the heart — but you didn't see the deed being done.

Your mind's eye had to show you the blood. You had to imagine the vampire crumbling away into dust and bones as the rays of the sun hit him.

But times change. Things that couldn't be shown in a movie in 1931 no longer seemed so frightening 25 years later. In 1958, an English company, Hammer Films, brought out a new version of Bram Stoker's Dracula.

It left little to the imagination.

The star of the Hammer film, Dracula, was Christopher Lee. He gave the evil count a new image that struck terror even into modern day hearts.

Dracula, in living color, had red eyes that gleamed in the dark. His fanged teeth dripped blood. He did not play the role as Bela Lugosi had. Instead, he leaped upon his victims like a wild beast. He was strong and irresistible to his victims. Somehow, you knew he hated himself for what he was. At the same time he loved being a vampire. He didn't do anything so silly as turn into a bat. He was horrible enough just as he was!

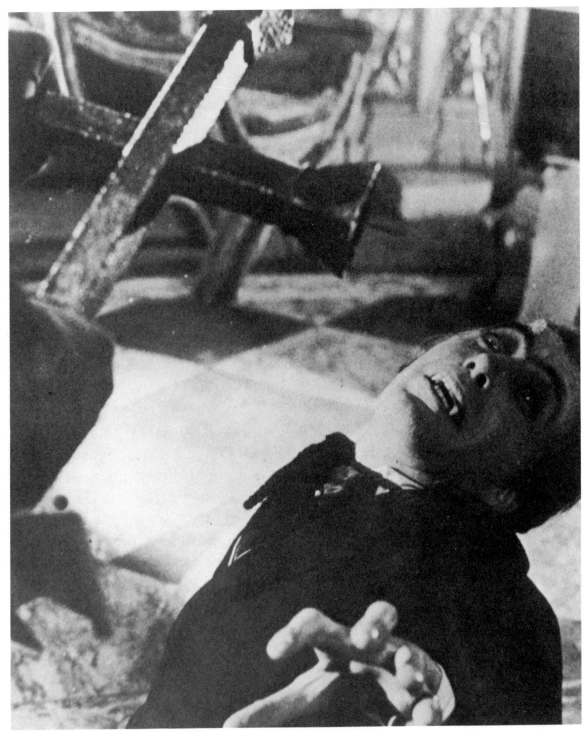

Two crossed candlesticks repel Dracula.

Horror of Dracula was not a movie for those who were easily frightened. It was a masterpiece of nightmare.

At the end, Dracula fought with Van Helsing. The professor escaped the vampire's clutches. He made a flying leap at a nearby window and ripped down the heavy drapes.

Sunlight flooded the castle and struck Dracula. In a last, horrid scene, the vampire turned into dust, crumbling as Van Helsing watched.

Hammer made many other vampire films starring Christopher Lee. However, none of them was as effective as Horror of Dracula.

The vampire disintegrates in the sunlight.

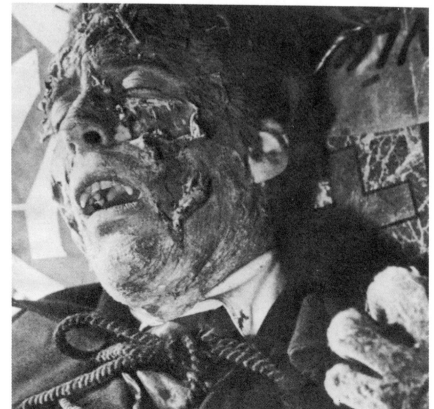

Have you ever been frightened by a strange noise in a dark house? (Everybody has.)

When you discovered the noise was just a shade rattling in the wind, or some other harmless thing, you laughed out loud.

You laugh at yourself for being scared. The thing that once frightened you becomes funny.

Movie monsters have become funny in somewhat the same way. The first of the monster comedies was a 1948 classic, Abbott and Costello Meet Frankenstein. In it, two comics try to escape from Frankenstein's monster, Dracula, and the Wolf Man. The resulting mix of horror and humor created a wonderful movie.

Comical Lou Costello is no match for Lugosi's Dracula in **Abbott and Costello Meet Frankenstein.**

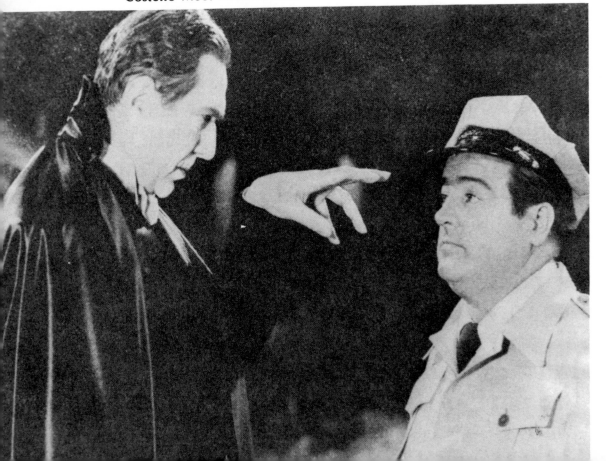

Al Lewis as lovable old Grandpa Dracula in "The Munsters."

By the 1960's, Dracula had become so tame he was featured in a television comedy series, "The Munsters." Dracula, having lost most of his evil powers, is now the lovable Grandpa of the odd Munster family.

The once fearful vampire now spent his time puttering in a lab, doing magic tricks that rarely worked properly, and playing with his pet bat, Igor. It was pretty funny but quite different from the days when Dracula's name struck terror into the hearts of young and old.

Fortunately, many people enjoy a good scare. This is why horror movies are so popular. The lovable monster craze of the 1960's faded away and, once again, evil vampires returned to the screen.

One of the most interesting modern vampire films was Blacula (1972). Stage actor William Marshall played an African prince, Mamuwalde, who was turned into a vampire by Dracula himself.

The prince's coffin was taken to California. There the black vampire revived and went looking for human blood.

Mamuwalde was a different type of vampire. He could not help seeking victims, but he was also capable of love. One beautiful woman, the image of his long-dead wife, returned Mamuwalde's love. She fled with him as the police closed in on the vampire.

A bullet meant for Mamuwalde killed his loved one instead. Enraged, the black prince destroyed the police then walked into the sunlight on purpose which doomed him.

Blacula was a success, largely due to the great acting of William Marshall. A weaker film Scream, Blacula, Scream, continued the story about the vampire prince, Mamuwalde.

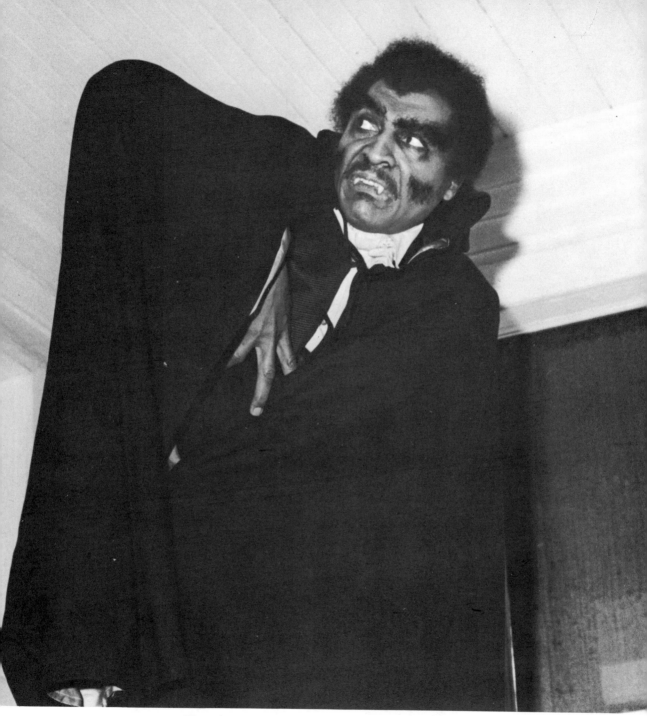

Blacula was portrayed by William Marshall.

Modern vampire movies have given the old monsters a new look. There are no more tumbledown castles, foggy moors, or spider webs. Instead, the vampire is usually shown doing his terrible deeds in a modern city.

Count Yorga, Vampire, starred handsome Robert Quarry in the title role. He sought his victims in Los Angeles. After killing all the main characters, Count Yorga escaped. The Return of Count Yorga saw the evil hero as the leader of a whole horde of vampires. In the end, the fanged mob is overcome by the valiant Dr. Baldwin. The lovely Cynthia, who loved Yorga, turns gratefully to Baldwin, who has rescued her.

At the end of the film, Baldwin smiles revealing his own set of gleaming fangs!

Count Yorga, Vampire, dies with a stake in the heart. Film writers can't seem to agree on the best way to kill vampires.

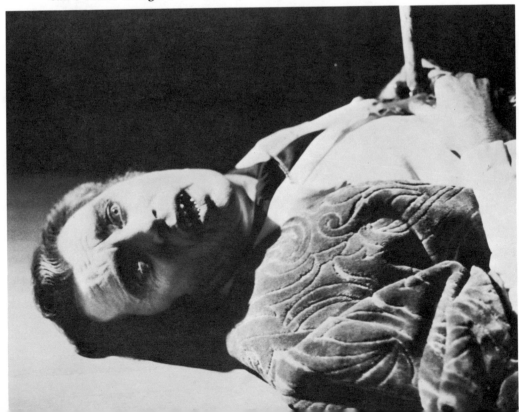

Vampirish folk close in on Charlton Heston in **The Omega Man.**

Science fiction author Richard Matheson wrote a terrifying novel, I Am Legend, about a whole race of vampires. A disease had caused everyone but the hero to become vampire-like monsters.

Two movies were made from this novel: The Last Man on Earth (1964), starring Vincent Price; and The Omega Man (1974), starring Charleton Heston. Neither movie was as frightening as the original book.

Barry Atwater was the vampire in **The Night Stalker.**

One of the best vampire films ever made was The Night Stalker, from a story by Jeff Rice. It was written and produced for television in 1972 by Richard Matheson.

The hero of the story was a seedy newspaper reporter named Kolchak. He investigated some strange deaths in which the victims were drained of blood. Kolchak was certain the killings were done by a vampire and tried to tell his editor and the police that a fanged monster was stalking the streets of Las Vegas.

Of course, nobody believed him.

Darren McGavin played Kolchak who was bumbling, funny, even sad with helplessness. The vampire, Janos Skorzeny, was played by Barry Atwater who never spoke a word during the entire film.

Poor Kolchak tried without success to tell others that Skorzeny was a genuine vampire. But everyone knew that vampires just don't exist! So Kolchak, alone and scared to death, had to overcome the monster himself and save Las Vegas from the modern day Dracula.

The Night Stalker received the highest ratings of any movie made for TV. It was a masterpiece, and it is still seen in re-runs today.

Darren McGavin hopes that crosses really repel vampires.

Almost all movies about vampires (except Blacula) showed the undead as cruel and evil. Author Richard Matheson tried to show a more human, tragic Dracula in a TV movie made in 1974. Jack Palance played the title role with dignity and power.

Matheson's Dracula was actually Vlad Tepes. The prince was condemned to remain undead because of his monstrous crimes. A touching scene showed Dracula as a young man, 500 years before, with his beloved Maria.

Dracula, played by Jack Palance, cannot help turning his love into a vampire like himself.

A modern day girl, Lucy, resembled Maria. Dracula fell in love with her but could not overcome his vampire desires. He turned Lucy into one of the undead — only to lose her again when Van Helsing put a stake into her heart.

At the movie's end, Dracula is destroyed by sunlight and one of Vlad's impaling stakes. He dies with a look of relief on his face. And we know that the terrible Prince of Transylvania has found peace at last.

MONSTERS

I SUGGEST YOU READ ABOUT MY FRIENDS!

THE BLOB
DRACULA
GODZILLA
KING KONG
THE MUMMY
FRANKENSTEIN
MAD SCIENTISTS
THE WOLF MAN
THE DEADLY MANTIS
THE INVISIBLE MAN
IT CAME FROM OUTER SPACE
THE PHANTOM OF THE OPERA
FRANKENSTEIN MEETS WOLFMAN
THE MURDERS IN THE RUE MORGUE
CREATURE FROM THE BLACK LAGOON

CRESTWOOD HOUSE